*There is a treasure that delights
and enriches beyond gold or silver:
the treasure of a great story.
Walker Treasures are exquisite
editions of some of the world's
greatest stories – both well-loved
favourites and little-known gems –
each illustrated by one of today's
finest picture-book artists.
A pleasure not only to look at
and read, but also to hold, these
are classic works of literature to
collect and to keep for ever.*

*The key to this Treasure is yours.
Open it and enjoy the riches
that lie within.*

THE
LORD FISH

WALTER
DE LA MARE

ILLUSTRATED BY

PATRICK BENSON

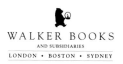

WALKER BOOKS
AND SUBSIDIARIES

LONDON · BOSTON · SYDNEY

Walter de la Mare (1873–1956) wrote numerous works of fiction and poetry for both adults and children, and is generally considered to be one of the finest children's poets of the twentieth century. He received several major awards, including the James Tait Black Memorial Prize and the Carnegie Medal, and in 1948 he was made a Companion of Honour. His most acclaimed work for children was the poetry book, *Peacock Pie*, but de la Mare was also a master of the short story, drawing on traditional folk-lore as the starting point for magical tales such as *The Three Mulla-Mulgars* (later reissued as *The Three Royal Monkeys*) and *The Lord Fish*, which, according to the critic Margery Fisher, "may well be the best original fairy tale of this century".

Patrick Benson received the 1984 Mother Goose Award as the most exciting new children's book artist for his illustration of William Mayne's *Hob Stories*. Since then he has illustrated many titles, including *The Wind in the Willows* and William Horwood's sequel *The Willows in Winter*, Roald Dahl's *The Minpins*, Martin Waddell's *Owl Babies*, Jonathan London's *Let the Lynx Come In* and his own story *Little Penguin*. In 1995 he won the Kurt Maschler Award for *The Little Boat* (by Kathy Henderson), which was also shortlisted for the Smarties Book Prize and the Kate Greenaway Medal. Like John Cobbler, the hero of *The Lord Fish*, Patrick Benson has a passion for fishing. He lives in Dorset with his partner and young son.

ONCE UPON A TIME there lived in the village of Tussock in Wiltshire a young man called John Cobbler. Cobbler being his name, there must have been shoe-making in his family. But there had been none in John's lifetime; nor within living memory either. And John cobbled nothing but his own old shoes and his mother's. Still, he was a handy young man. He could have kept them both with ease and with plenty of butter to their bread, if only he had been a little different from what he was. He was lazy.

Lazy or not, his mother loved him dearly. She had loved him ever since he was a baby, when his chief joy was to suck his thumb and stare out of his saucer blue eyes at nothing in particular except what he had no words to tell about. Nor had John lost this habit, even when he was being a handy young man. He could make baskets – of sorts; he was a wonder with bees; he could mend pots and pans, if he were given the solder and could find his iron; he could grow cabbages, hoe potatoes, patch up a hen-house or limewash a sty. But he was only a jack of such trades, and master of none. He could seldom finish off anything; not at any rate as his namesake the Giant Killer could finish off his giants. He began well; he went on worse; and he ended, yawning. And unless his mother had managed to get a little washing and ironing and mending and sweeping and cooking and stitching from the gentry in the village, there would often have been less in the pot for them both than would keep their bodies and souls — and the two of them — together.

Yet even though John was by nature idle and a daydreamer, he might have made his mother far easier about his future if only he could have given up but one small pleasure and pastime; he might have made not only good wages, but also his fortune — even though he would have had to leave Tussock to do it quick. It was his love of water that might some day be his ruin. Or rather, not so much his love of water as his passion for fishing in it. Let him but catch sight of a puddle, or of rain gushing from a waterspout, or hear in the middle of the night a leaky tap singing its queer *ding-dong-bell* as drop followed drop into a basin in the sink, let the wind but creep an inch or two out of the east and into the south; and every other thought would instantly vanish out of his head. All he wanted then was a rod and a line and a hook and a worm and a cork; a pond or a stream or a river or the deep blue sea. And it wasn't even fish he pined for, merely fishing.

There would have been little harm in this craving of his if only he had been able to keep it within bounds. But he couldn't. He fished morning, noon, and even night. Through continually staring at a float, his eyes had come to be almost as round as one, and his elbows stood out like fins when he walked. The wonder was his blood had not turned to water. And though there are many kinds of tasty English fish, his mother at last grew very tired of having *any* kind at every meal.

As the old rhyme goes:

A Friday of fish
Is all man could wish.
Of vittles the chief
Is mustard and beef.
It's only a glutton
Could live on cold mutton;
And bacon when green
Is too fat or too lean.
But all three are sweeter
To see in a dish
By any wise eater
Than nothing but FISH!

Quite a little fish, too, even a roach, may take as many hours to catch and almost as many minutes to cook as a full-sized one; and they both have the same number of bones. Still, in spite of his fish *and* his fishing, his mother went

on loving her son John. She hoped in time he might weary of them himself. Or was there some secret in his passion for water of which she knew nothing? Might he some day fish up something really worth having – something to keep? A keg perhaps of rubies and diamonds, or a coffer full of amber and gold? Then all their troubles would be over.

Meanwhile John showed no sign at all of becoming less lazy or of growing tired of fishing, though he was no longer content to fish in the same places. He would walk miles and miles in hope to find pond, pool or lake that he had never seen before, or a stream strange to him. Wherever he heard there was water within reach between dawn and dark, off he would go to look for it. Sometimes in his journeyings he would do a job of work, and bring home to his mother not only a few pence but a little present for herself − a ribbon, or a needlecase, a bag of jumbles or bull's-eyes, or a duck's egg for her tea; any little thing that might take her fancy. Sometimes the fish he caught in far-off waters tasted fresher, sweeter, richer, juicier than those from nearer home; sometimes they tasted worse − dry, poor, rank and muddy. It depended partly on the sort of fish, partly on how long he had taken to carry them home, and partly on how his mother felt at the moment.

Now there was a stream John Cobbler came to hear about which for a long time he could never find. For whenever he went to look for it — and he knew that it lay a good fourteen miles and more from Tussock — he was always baulked by a high flintstone wall. It was the highest wall he had ever seen. And, like the Great Wall of China, it went on for miles. What was more curious, although he had followed the wall on and on for hours at a stretch, he had never yet been able to find a gate or door to it, or any way in.

When he asked any stranger

whom he happened to meet at such times if he knew what lay on the other side of this mysterious wall, and whether there were any good fish in the stream which he had been told ran there, and if so, of what kind, shape, size and flavour they might be – every single one of them told him a different tale. Some said there was a castle inside the wall, a good league or so away from it, and that a sorcerer lived in it who had mirrors on a tower in which he could detect any stranger that neared his walls. Others said an old, old Man of the Sea had built himself a great land mansion there in the middle of a Maze – of water and yew trees; an old Man of the Sea who had turned cannibal, and always drowned anybody who trespassed over his wall before devouring him. Others said water-witches dwelt there, in a wide lake made by the stream beside the ruinous walls of a palace which had been the abode of princes in old times. All agreed that it was a dangerous place, and that they would not venture over the wall, dark or daylight, for a pocketful of guineas. On summer nights, they said, you could hear voices coming from away over it, very strange voices, too; and would see lights in the sky. And some avowed they had heard hunting-horns at the rise of the moon. As for the fish, all agreed they must be monsters.

There was no end to the tales told John of what lay beyond the wall. And he, being a simple young man, believed each one of them in turn. But none made any difference to the longing that had come over him to get to the other side of this wall and to fish in the stream there. Walls that kept out so much, he thought, must keep something well worth having *in*. All other fishing now seemed tame and dull. His only hope was to find out the secret of what lay beyond this high, grey, massive, mossy, weed-tufted, endless wall. And he stopped setting out in its direction only for the sake of his mother.

But though for this reason he might stay at home two or three days together, the next would see him off again, hungering for the unknown waters.

John not only thought of the

wall all day, he dreamed of it and of what might be beyond it by night. If the wind sighed at his window he saw moonlit lakes and water in his sleep; if a wild duck cried over head under the stars, there would be thousands of wild duck and wild swans too and many another water-bird haunting his mind, his head on his pillow. Sometimes great whales would come swimming into his dreams. And he would hear mermaids blowing in their hollow shells and singing as they combed their hair.

With all this longing he began to pine away a little. His eye grew less clear and lively. His rib-bones began to show. And though his mother saw a good deal more of her son John since he had given up his fishing, at last she began to miss more and more and more what she had become accustomed to. Fish, that is – boiled, broiled, baked, fried or Dutch-ovened. And her longing came to such a pass at last that she laid down her knife and fork one supper-time beside a half-eaten slice of salt pork and said, "My! John, how I would enjoy a morsel of tench again! Do you remember those tench you used to catch up at Abbot's Pool? Or a small juicy trout, John! Or some stewed eels! Or even a few roach out of the moat of the old Grange, even though they *are* mostly mud! It's funny, John, but sea-fish never did satisfy me even when we could get it; and I haven't scarcely any fancy left for meat.

What's more, I notice cheese now gives you nightmares. But fish? – never!"

This was enough for John. For weeks past he had been sitting on the see-saw of his mind, so that just the least little tilt like that bumped him clean into a decision. It was not fear or dread indeed, all this talk of giants and wizardry and old bygone princes that had kept him from scaling the great wall long ago, and daring the dangers beyond it. It was not this at all. But only a half-hidden feeling in his mind that if once he found himself on the other side of it he might never be quite the same creature again. You may get out of your bed in the morning, the day's usual sunshine at the window and the birds singing as they always sing, and yet know for certain that in the hours to come something is going to happen – something that hasn't happened before. So it was with John Cobbler. At the very moment his mother put down her knife and fork on either side of her half-eaten slice of salt pork and said, "My! John, how I would enjoy a morsel of tench again! … or a small juicy trout, John!" his mind was made up.

"Why, of course, Mother dear," he said to her, in a voice that he tried in vain to keep from trembling. "I'll see what I can do for you tomorrow." He lit his candle there and then, and scarcely able to breathe for joy at thought of it, clumped up the wooden stairs to his attic to look out his best rod and get ready his tackle.

While yet next morning the

eastern sky was pale blue with the early light of dawn, wherein tiny clouds like a shoal of silver fishes were quietly drifting on – before, that is, the flaming sun had risen, John was posting along out of Tussock with his rod and tackle and battered old creel, and a hunk of bread and cheese tied up in a red spotted handkerchief. There was not a soul to be seen. Every blind was down; the chimneys were empty of smoke; the whole village was still snoring. He whistled as he walked, and every now and again took a look at the sky. That vanishing fleecy drift of silver fishes might mean wind, and from the south, he thought. He plodded along to such good purpose, and without meeting a soul except a

shepherd with his sheep and dog
and an urchin driving a handful
of cows — for these were solitary
parts — that he came to the wall
while it was still morning, and
a morning as fresh and green as
ever England can show.

Now John wasn't making merely
for the wall, but for a certain place
in it. It was where, one darkening
evening some little time before,
he had noticed the still-sprouting
upper branches of a tree that had
been blown down in a great wind
over the edge of the wall and into

the narrow grassy lane that skirted it. Few humans seemed ever to come this way, but there were hosts of rabbits, whose burrows were in the sandy hedgerow, and, at evening, nightjars, croodling in the dusk. It was too, John had noticed, a favourite resort of bats.

After a quick look up and down the lane to see that the coast was clear, John stood himself under the dangling branches – like the fox in the fable that was after the grapes – and he jumped, and jumped. But no matter how high he jumped, the lowermost twigs remained out of his reach. He rested awhile looking about him, and spied a large stone half-buried in the sandy hedgerow. He trundled it over until it was under the tree, and after a third attempt succeeded in swinging himself up into its branches, and had scrambled along and dropped quietly in on the other side almost before news of his coming had spread among the wild things that lived on the other side of it. Then blackbird to blackbird sounded the alarm. There was a scurry and scamper among the leaves and bracken. A host of rooks rose cawing into the sky. Then all was still. John peered about him; he had never felt so lonely in his life. Never even in his dreams had he been in a place so strange to him as this. The foxgloves and bracken of its low hills and hollows showed bright green where the sunshine struck through the great forest trees. Else, so dense with leaves were their branches that for the most part there was only an emerald twilight beneath their boughs. And a deep silence dwelt there.

For some little time John walked steadily on, keeping his eyes open as he went. Near and far he heard jays screaming one to the other, and woodpigeons went clattering up out of the leaves into the sun. Ever and again, too, the hollow tapping of a woodpecker sounded out in the silence, or its wild echoing laughter, and once he edged along a glade just in time to see a herd of deer fleeting in a multitude before him at sight and scent of man. They sped soundlessly out of view across the open glade into covert. And still John kept steadily on, lifting his nose every now and again to snuff the air; for his fisherman's wits had hinted that water was near.

And he came at length to a gentle slope waist-high with spicy bracken, and at its crest found himself looking down on the waters of a deep and gentle stream flowing between its hollow mossy banks in the dingle below him. "Aha!" cried John out loud to himself; and the sound of his voice rang so oddly in the air that he whipped round and stared about him as if someone else had spoken. But there was sign neither of man nor bird nor beast. All was still again. So he cautiously made his way down to the bank of the stream and began to fish.

For an hour or more he fished in vain. The trees grew thicker on the further bank, and the water was deep and dark and slow. Nonetheless, though he could see none, he knew in his bones that it was fairly alive with fish. Yet not a single one of them had as yet cheated him even with a nibble. Still, John had often fished half a day through without getting so much as a bite, and so long as the water stole soundlessly on beneath him and he could watch the reflection of the tree boughs and of the drifts of blue sky between them in this dark looking-glass, he was happy and at ease. And then suddenly, as if to mock him, a fish with a dappled green back and silver belly and of a kind he never remembered to have seen before, leapt clean out of the water about three yards from his green and white float, seemed to stare at him a moment with fishy lidless eyes, and at once plunged back into the

water again. Whether it was the mere noise of its watersplash, or whether the words had actually sounded from out of its gaping jaws he could not say, but it certainly seemed as if before it vanished he had heard a strange voice cry, "Ho, there! John! – Try lower down!"

He laughed to himself; then listened. Biding a bit, he clutched his rod a little tighter, and keeping a more cautious look-out than ever on all sides of him, he followed the flow of the water, pausing every now and again to make a cast. And still not a single fish seemed so much as to have sniffed (or even sneered) at his bait, while yet the gaping mouths of those leaping up out of the water beyond his reach seemed

to utter the same hollow and watery-sounding summons he had heard before: "Ho, John! Ho! Ho, you, John Cobbler, there! Try lower down!" So much indeed were these fish like fish enchanted, that John began to wish he had kept to his old haunts and had not ventured over the wall; or that he had at least told his mother where he meant to go. Supposing he never came back? Where would she be looking for him? Where? Where? And all she had asked for, and perhaps for his own sake only, was a fish supper!

The water was now flowing more rapidly in a glass-green heavy flood and, before he was ready for it, John suddenly found himself staring up at the walls of a high dark house with but two narrow windows in the stone surface that steeped up into the sky above. And the very sight of the house set his heart beating faster. He was afraid. Beyond this wall to the right showed the stony roofs of lesser buildings, and moss-clotted fruit trees gone to leaf. Busying to and fro above the roof were scores of rooks and jackdaws, their jangled cries sounding out even above the roaring of the water, for now close beneath him the stream narrowed to gush in beneath a low rounded arch in the wall, and so into the silence and darkness beyond it.

Two thoughts had instantly sprung up in John's mind as he stared up at this strange solitary house. One that it must be bewitched, and the other that except for its birds and the fish in its stream it was forsaken and empty. He laid his rod down on the green bank and stole from one tree-trunk to another to get a better view, making up his mind that if he had time he would skirt his way round the walled garden he could see, but would not yet venture to walk out into the open on the other side of the house.

It was marvellously quiet in this dappled sunshine, and John decided to rest awhile before venturing further. Seating himself

under a tree he opened his handkerchief, and found not only the
hunk of bread and cheese he had
packed in it, but a fat sausage
and some cockled apples which
his mother must have put in
afterwards. He was uncommonly
hungry, and keeping a wary eye
on the two dark windows from
under the leaves over his head,
he continued to munch. And as
he munched, the jackdaws, their
black wings silvered by the sun,
continued to jangle, and the fish
silently to leap up out of their
watery haunts and back again,
their eyes glassily fixed on him

as they did so, and the gathering water continued to gush steadily in under the dark rounded tunnel beneath the walls of the house.

But now as John listened and watched he fancied that above all these sounds interweaving themselves into a gentle chorus of the morning, he caught the faint strains as of a voice singing in the distance – and a sweet voice too. But water, as he knew of old, is a curious deceiver of the ear. At times, as one listens to it, it will sound as if drums and dulcimers are ringing in its depths; at times as if fingers are plucking on the strings of a harp, or invisible mouths calling. John stopped eating to listen more intently.

And soon there was no doubt left in his mind that this was no mere water noise, but the singing of a human voice, and that not far away. It came as if from within the walls of the house itself, but he could not detect any words to the song. It glided on from note to note as though it were an unknown bird piping in the first cold winds of April after its sea-journey from Africa to English shores; and though he did not know it, his face as he listened puckered up almost as if he were a child again and was going to cry.

He had heard tell of the pitiless sirens, and of sea-wandering nereids, and of how they sing among their island rocks, or couched on the oceanic strands of their sunny islands, where huge sea-fish disport themselves in the salt water: porpoise and dolphin, through billows clear as glass, and green and blue as precious stones. His mother too had told him as a child – and like Simple Simon himself he had started fishing in her pail! – what dangers there may be in listening to such voices; how even sailors have stopped up their ears with wax lest they should be enticed by this music to the isles of the sirens and never sail home again. But though John remembered this warning, he continued to listen, and an intense desire came over him to discover who this secret singer was, and where she lay hid. He might peep perhaps, he thought to himself, through some lattice or cranny in the dark walls and not be seen.

But though he stole on, now in shadow, now in sun, pushing his way through the tangled brambles and briars, the bracken and bryony that grew close in even under the walls of the house, he found — at least on this side of it — no doorway or window or even slit in the masonry through which to look in. And he came back at last, hot, tired and thirsty, to the bank of the stream where he had left his rod.

And even as he knelt down to drink by the waterside, the voice which had been silent awhile began to sing again, as sad as it was sweet; and not more than an arm's length from his stooping face a great fish leapt out of the water, its tail bent almost double, its goggling eyes fixed on him, and out of its hook-toothed mouth it cried, *"A-whoof! Oo-ougoolkawott!"*

That at least to John was what it seemed to say. And having delivered its message, it fell back again into the dark water and in a wild eddy was gone. Startled by this sudden noise John drew quickly back, and in so doing dislodged a large moss-greened stone on the bank, which rolled clattering down to its plunge into the stream; and the singing again instantly ceased. He glanced back over his shoulder at the high wall and vacant windows, and, out of the silence that had again descended, he heard in midday the mournful hooting as of an owl, and a cold terror swept over him. He leapt to his feet, seized his rod and creel, hastily tied up what was left of his lunch in his red spotted handkerchief, and instantly set out for home. Nor did he once look back until the house was hidden from view. Then his fear vanished, and he began to be heartily ashamed of himself.

And since he had by now come into sight of another loop of the stream, he decided, however long it took him, to fish there until he had at least caught *something* − if only a stickleback − so that he should not disappoint his mother of the supper she longed for. The minnow smeared with pork marrow which he had been using for bait on his hook was already dry. Nonetheless he flung it into the stream, and almost before the float touched the water a swirl of ripples came sweeping from the further bank, and a greedy pike, grey and silver, at least two feet

long if he was an inch, had
instantly gobbled down bait and
hook. John could hardly believe
his own eyes. It was as if it had
been actually lying in wait to be
caught. He stooped to look into
its strange motionless eye as it lay
on the grass at his feet. Sullenly it
stared back at him as though, even
if it had only a minute or two left
to live in, it were trying heroically

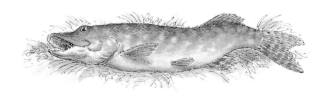

to give him a message, yet one
that he could not understand.

Happy at heart, he stayed no
longer. Yet with every mile of his
journey home the desire grew in

him to return to the house, if only to hear again that dolorous voice singing from out of the darkness within its walls. But he told his mother nothing about his adventures, and the two of them sat down to as handsome a dish of fish for supper as they had ever tasted.

"What's strange to me, John," said his mother at last, for they had talked very little, being so hungry, "is that though this fish here is a pike, and cooked as usual, with a picking of thyme and marjoram, a bit of butter, a squeeze of lemon and some chopped shallots, there's a good deal more to him than just that. There's a sort of savour and sweetness to him, as if he had been daintily fed. Where did you catch him, John?"

But at this question John was

seized by such a fit of coughing –
as if a bone had stuck in his throat
– that it seemed at any moment
he might choke. And when his
mother had stopped thumping
him on his back she had forgotten what she had asked him.
With her next mouthful, too, she
had something else to think about;
and it was fortunate that she had
such a neat strong row of teeth,
else the crunch she gave to it
would certainly have broken two
or three of them in half.

"Excuse me, John," she said, and
drew out of her mouth not a
bone, but something tiny, hard
and shiny, which after being
washed under the kitchen tap
proved to be a key. It was etched
over with figures of birds and
beasts and fishes, that might be

all ornament or
might, thought John,
his cheeks red as
beetroot, be a secret
writing.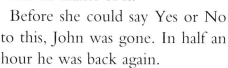

"Well I never! Brass,"
said his mother, staring
at the key in the palm
of her hand.

"Nor didn't I," said
John. "I'll take it off
to the blacksmith's at
once, Mother, and see
what he makes of it."

Before she could say Yes or No
to this, John was gone. In half an
hour he was back again.

"He says, Mother," said he, "it's
a key, Mother; and not brass but
solid gold. A gold key! Whoever?
And in a fish!"

"Well, John," said his mother,

who was a little sleepy after so
hearty a supper, "I never – mind
you – did see much good in
fishing except the fish, but if there
are any more gold keys from
where that pike came from, let's
both get up early, and we'll soon
be as rich as Old Creatures."

John needed no telling. He was
off next morning long before
the sun had begun to gild the
dewdrops in the meadows, and
he found himself, rod, creel
and bait, under the magician's
wall a good three hours before
noon. There was not a cloud in
the sky. The stream flowed quiet
as molten glass, reflecting the
towering forest trees, the dark
stone walls, and the motionless
flowers and grassblades at its brim.
John stood there gazing awhile

into the water, just as if today were yesterday over again, then sat himself down on the bank and fell into a kind of daydream, his rod idle at his side. Neither fish nor key nor the freshness of the morning nor any wish or thought was in his mind but only a longing to hear again the voice of the secret one. And the shadows around him had crept less even than an inch on their daily round, and a cuckoo under the hollow sky had but thrice cuckoo'd in some green dell of the forest, when there slid up into the air the very notes that had haunted him, waking and sleeping, ever since they had first fallen on his ear. They rang gently on and on, in the hush, clear as a cherub in some quiet gallery of paradise, and John knew in his heart that she who sang was no longer timid in his company, but out of her solitude was beseeching his aid.

He rose to his feet, and once more searched the vast frowning walls above his head. Nothing there but the croaking choughs and jackdaws among the chimneys, and a sulphur-coloured butterfly wavering in flight along the darkness of their stones. They filled him with dread, these echoing walls; and still the voice pined on. And at last he fixed his eyes on the dark arch beneath which coursed in heavy leaden flow the heaped-up volume of the stream. No way in, indeed! Surely, where water could go, mightn't *he*?

Without waiting a moment to

consider the dangers that might lie in wait for him in the dark water beneath the walls, he had slipped out of his coat and shoes and had plunged in. He swam on with the stream until he was within a little way of the yawning arch; then took a deep breath and dived down and down. When he could hold it no longer he slipped up out of the water — and in the nick of time. He had clutched something as he came to the surface, and found himself in a dusky twilight looking up from the foot of a narrow flight of stone steps — with a rusty chain dangling down the middle of it. He hauled himself up out of the water and sat down a moment to recover his breath, then made his way up the steps. At the top he

came to a low stone corridor.
There he stayed again.

But here the voice was more
clearly to be heard. He hastened
down the corridor and came at
last to a high narrow room full of
sunlight from the window in its
walls looking out over the forest.
And, reclining there by the
window, the wan green light
shining in on her pale face and
plaited copper-coloured hair, was
what John took at first to be a
mermaid; and for the very good
reason that she had a human head
and body, but a fish's tail. He
stayed quite still, gazing at her, and
she at him, but he could think of
nothing to say. He merely kept his
mouth open in case any words
should come, while the water-
drops dripped from his clothes and

hair on to the stone flags around him. And when the lips in the odd small face of this strange creature began to speak to him, he could hardly make head or tail of the words. Indeed she had been long shut up alone in this old mansion from which the magician – who had given her her fish's tail, so that she should not be able to stray from the house – had some years gone his way, never to come back. She had now almost forgotten her natural language. But there is a music in the voice that tells more to those who understand it than can any words in a dictionary. And it didn't take John very long to discover that this poor fish-tailed creature, with nothing but the sound of her own sad voice to comfort her, was mortally unhappy; that all she longed for was to rid herself of her cold fish's tail, and so win out into the light and sunshine again, freed from the spell of the wizard who had shut her up in these stone walls.

John sat down on an old wooden stool that stood beside the table, and listened. And now and then he himself sighed deep or nodded. He learned – though he learned it very slowly – that the only company she had was a deaf old steward who twice every day, morning and evening, brought her food and water, and for the rest of the time shut himself up in a tower on the further side of the house looking out over the deserted gardens and orchards that once had flourished with peach and quince and apricot, and all the roses of Damascus. Else, she said, sighing, she was always alone. And John, as best he could, told her in turn about himself and about his mother. "She'd help you all she could to escape away from here — I know *that*, if so be she *could*. The only question is, How? Since, you see, first it's a good long step for Mother to come and there's no proper way over the wall, and next if she managed it, it wouldn't be easy with nothing but a tail to walk on. I mean, lady, for you to walk on." At this he left his mouth open, and looked away, afraid that he might have hurt her feelings. And in the same moment he bethought himself of the key, which, if he had not been on the verge of choking, his mother might have swallowed in mistake for a mouthful of fish. He took it out of his breeches' pocket and held it up towards the window, so that the light should shine on it. And, at sight of it, it seemed that something between grief and gladness had suddenly overcome the poor creature with the fish's tail, for she hid her face in her fingers and wept aloud.

This was not much help to poor John. With his idle ways and love of fishing, he had been a sad trial at times to his mother. But she, though little to look at, was as brave as a lion, and if ever she shed tears at all, it was in secret. This perhaps was a pity, for if John had but once seen her cry he might have known what to do now. All that he actually did do was to look very glum himself and turn his eyes away. And as they roved slowly round the bare walls he perceived what looked like the crack of a little door in the stones and beside it a tiny keyhole. The one thing in the world he craved was to comfort this poor damsel with the fish's tail, to persuade her to dry her eyes and smile at him. But as nothing he could think to say could be of any help, he tiptoed across and examined the wall more closely. And cut into the stone above the keyhole he read the four letters − C.A.V.E.! What they meant John had no notion, except that a cave is something hollow − and usually empty. Still, since here was a lock and John had a key, he naturally put the key into the lock with his clumsy fingers to see if it would

fit. He gave the key a gentle twist.
And lo and behold, there came a
faint click. He tugged, drew the
stone out upon its iron hinges, and
looked inside.

What he had expected to see he
did not know. All that was actually
within this narrow stone cupboard

was a little green pot, and beside
it a scrap of what looked like
parchment, but was actually
monkey skin. John had never
been much of a scholar at his
books. He was a dunce. When he
was small he had liked watching
the clouds and butterflies and
birds flitting to and fro and the
green leaves twinkling in the sun,
and found frogs and newts and

sticklebacks and minnows better company than anything he could read in print on paper. Still he had managed at last to learn all his letters and even to read, though he read so slowly that he sometimes forgot the first letters of a long word before he had spelled out the last. He took the piece of parchment into the light, held it tight between his fingers, and, syllable by syllable, muttered over to himself what it said – leaving the longer words until he had more time.

And now the pale-cheeked creature reclining by the window had stopped weeping, and between the long strands of her copper hair was watching him through her tears. And this is what John read:

Thou who wouldst dare
To free this Fair
From fish's shape,
And yet escape
O'er sea and land
My vengeful hand: –
Smear this fish-fat on thy heart,
And prove thyself the jack thou art!

With tail and fin
Then plunge thou in!
And thou shalt surely have thy wish
To see the great, the good Lord Fish!

Swallow his bait in haste, for he
Is master of all wizardry.
And if he gentle be inclined,
He'll show thee where to seek
  and find
The Magic Unguent that did make
This human maid a fish tail take.

But have a care
To make short stay
Where wields his sway,
The Great Lord Fish;
'Twill be too late
To moan your fate
When served with sauce
Upon his dish!

John read this doggerel once, he read it twice, and though he couldn't understand it all even when he read it a third time, he understood a good deal of it. The one thing he could not discover, though it seemed the most important, was what would happen to him if he did as the rhyme itself bade him do – smeared the fish-fat over his heart. But this he meant to find out.

And why not at once, thought John, though except when he hooked a fish, he was seldom as prompt as that. He folded up the parchment very small, and slipped it into his breeches' pocket. Then imitating as best he could the motion of descending the steps and diving into the water, he promised the maid he would return to her the first moment he could, and entreated her not to sing again until he came back. "Because…" he began, but could get no further. At which, poor mortal, she began to weep again, making John, for very sadness to see her, only the more anxious to be gone. So he took the little pot out of the stone cupboard, and giving her for farewell as smiling and consoling a bob of his head as he knew how, hurried off along the long narrow corridor, and so down the steep stone steps to the water.

There, having first very carefully felt with his fingertips exactly where his heart lay beating, he dipped his finger into the green ointment and rubbed it over his ribs. And with that, at once, a dreadful darkness and giddiness swept over him. He felt his body narrowing and shortening and shrinking and dwindling. His bones were drawing themselves together inside his skin; his arms and legs ceased at last to wave and scuffle, his eyes seemed to be settling into his head. The next moment, with one convulsive twist of his whole body, he had fallen plump into the water. There he lay a while in a motionless horror. Then he began to stir again, and after a few black dreadful moments found himself coursing along so swiftly that in a trice he was out from under the arch and into the green gloaming of the stream beyond it. Never before had he slipped through the water with such ease. And no wonder!

For when he twisted himself about to see what had happened to him, a sight indeed met his eye. Where once had been arms were now small blunt fins. A gristly little beard or barbel hung on either side of his mouth. His short dumpy body was of a greeny brown, and for human legs he could boast of nothing now but a fluted wavering tail. If he had been less idle in his young days he might have found himself a fine mottled trout, a barbel, a mullet, or a lively eel, or being a John he might well have become a jack. But no, he was fisherman enough to recognize himself at sight – a common tench, and not a very handsome one either! A mere middling fish, John judged. At this horrifying discovery, though the rhyme should have warned him of it, shudder after shudder ran along his backbone and he dashed blindly through the water as if he were out of his senses. Where could he hide himself? How flee away? What would his mother say to him? And alackaday, what had become of the pot of ointment? "Oh mercy me, oh misery me!" he moaned within himself, though not the faintest whisper sounded from his bony jaws. A pretty bargain this!

He plunged on deeper and deeper, and at length, nuzzling softly the sandy bed of the stream with his blunt fish's snout, he hid his head between two boulders at the bottom. There, under a net of bright green waterweed, he lay for a while utterly still, brooding again on his mother and on what her feelings would be if she should see him no more − or in the shape he was! Would that he had listened to her counsel, and had never so much as set eyes on rod or hook or line or float or water. He had wasted his young days in fishing, and now was fish for evermore.

But as the watery moments sped by, this grief and despondency

began to thin away and remembrance of the crafty and cruel magician came back to mind. Whatever he might look like from outside, John began to be himself again within. Courage, even a faint gleam of hope, welled back into his dull fish's brains. With a flick of his tail he had drawn back out of the gloomy cranny between the boulders, and was soon disporting himself but a few inches below the surface of the stream, the sunlight gleaming golden on his scales, the cold blood coursing through his body, and but one desire in his heart.

These high spirits indeed almost proved the end of him. For at this moment a prowling and hungry pike having from its hiding-place spied this plump young tench, came flashing through the water like an arrow from a bow, and John escaped the snap of its sharp-toothed jaws by less than half an inch. And when on land he had always supposed that the tench who is the fishes' doctor was safe from any glutton! After this dizzying experience he swam on more heedfully, playing a kind of hide-and-seek among the stones and weeds, and nibbling every now and again at anything he found to his taste. And the world of trees and sky in which but a few hours before he had walked about on his two human legs was a very strange thing to see from out of the rippling and distorting wavelets of the water.

When evening began to darken overhead he sought out what

seemed to be a safe lair for the night, and must soon have fallen into a long and peaceful fish's sleep – a queer sleep too, for having no lids to his eyes they both remained open, whereas even a hare when he is asleep shuts only one!

Next morning very early John was about again. A south wind must be blowing, he fancied, for there was a peculiar mildness and liveliness in the water, and he snapped at every passing titbit carried along by the stream with a zest and hunger that nothing could satisfy. Poor John, he had never dreamed a drowned fly or bee or a grub or caterpillar, or even waterweed, could taste so sweet. But then he had never tried to find out. And presently, dangling only a foot or two above his head, he espied a particularly juicy-looking and wriggling red worm.

Now though, as has been said already, John as a child or even as a small boy, had refrained from tasting caterpillars or beetles or snails or woodlice, he had once – when making mud pies in his mother's garden – nibbled at a little earthworm. But he had not nibbled much. For this reason only perhaps, he stayed eyeing this wriggling coral-coloured morsel above his head. Memory too had told him that it is not a habit of worms to float wriggling in the water like this. And though at sight of it he grew hungrier and hungrier as he finned softly on, he had the good sense to cast a glance up out of the water. And there – lank and lean upon the bank above – he perceived the strangest shape in human kind he had ever set eyes on. This bony old being had scarcely any shoulders. His grey glassy eyes bulged out of his head above his flat nose. A tuft of beard hung from his cod-like chin, and the hand that clutched his fishing rod was little else but skin and bone.

Now, thought John to himself, as he watched him steadily from out of the water, if that old rascal there ain't the Lord Fish in the rhyme, I'll eat my buttons. Which was an easy thing to promise, since at this moment John hadn't any buttons to eat.

It was by no means so easy to make up his hungry fishy mind to snap at the worm and chance what might come after. He longed beyond words to be home again; he longed beyond words to get back into his own body again – but only (and John seemed to be even stubborner as a fish than he had been as a human), *only* if the beautiful lady could be relieved of her tail. And how could there be hope of any of these things if he gave up this chance of meeting the Lord Fish and of finding the pot of "unguent" he had read of in the rhyme? The other had done its work with him quick enough!

If nothing had come to interrupt these cogitations, John might have cogitated too long. But a quick-eyed perch had at this moment finned into John's pool and had caught sight of the savoury morsel wriggling and waggling in the glass-clear water. At very first glimpse of him John paused no longer. With gaping jaws and one mad swirl of his fish tail he sprang at the worm. A dart of pain flashed through his body. He was whirled out of the water and into the air. He seemed on the point of suffocation. And the next instant found him gasping and floundering in the lush green grass that grew beside the water's brink. But the old angler who had

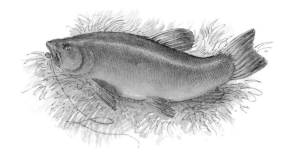

caught him was even more skilful in the craft of fishing than John Cobbler was himself. Almost before John could sob twice, the hook had been extracted from his mouth, he had been swathed up from head to tail in cool green moss, a noose had been slipped around that tail, and poor John, dangling head downwards from the fisherman's long skinny fingers, was being lugged away he knew not where. Few, fogged and solemn were the thoughts that passed through his gaping, gasping head on this dismal journey.

Now the Lord Fish who had caught him lived in a low stone house which was surrounded on three sides by a lake of water, and was not far distant from his master's — the Sorcerer. Fountains jetted in its hollow echoing chambers, and water lapped its walls on every side. Not even the barking of a fox or the scream of a peacock or any sound of birds could be heard in it; it was so full of the suffling and sighing, the music and murmuration of water, all day, all night long. But poor John being upside down had little opportunity to view or heed its marvels. And still muffled up in his thick green overcoat of moss he presently found himself suspended by his tail from a hook in the Lord Fish's larder, a long cool dusky room or vault with but one window to it, and that only a hole in the upper part of the wall. This larder too was of stone, and apart from other fish as luckless as John who hung there gaping from their hooks, many more, plumper and heavier than he, lay still and cold on the slate slab shelves around him. Indeed, if he could have done so, he might have hung his head a little lower at being so poor a fish by comparison.

Now there was a little maid who was in the service of this Lord Fish. She was the guardian of his larder. And early next morning she came in and set about her day's work. John watched her without ceasing. So fish-like was the narrow face that looked out from between the grey-green plaits of her hair that he could not even guess how old she was. She might, he thought, be twelve; she *might*, if age had not changed her much, be sixty. But he guessed she must be about seventeen. She was

not of much beauty to human eyes — so abrupt was the slope of her narrow shoulders, so skinny were her hands and feet.

First she swept out the larder with a besom and flushed it out with buckets of water. Then, with an earthenware watering pot, and each in turn, she sprinkled the moss and weed and grasses in which John and his fellows were enwrapped. For the Lord Fish, John soon discovered, devoured his fish raw, and liked them fresh. When one of them, especially of those on the shelves, looked more solemn and motionless than was good for him, she dipped him into a shallow trough of running water that lay outside the door of the larder. John indeed heard running water all day long — while he himself could scarcely flick a fin. And when all this was done, and it was done twice a day, the larder maid each morning chose out one or two or even three of her handsomest fish and carried them off with her. John knew – to his horror – to what end.

But there were two things that gave him heart and courage in this gruesome abode. The first was that after her second visit the larder maid treated him with uncommon kindness. Perhaps there was a look on his face not quite like that of her other charges. For John with his goggling ogling eyes would try to twist up his poor fish face into something of a smile when she came near him, and – though very faintly – to waggle his tail tips, as if in greeting. However that might be, there was no doubt she had taken a liking to him. She not only gave him more of her fishpap than she gave the rest, to fatten him up, but picked him out special dainties. She sprinkled him more slowly than the others with her waterpot so that he could enjoy the refreshment the more. And, after a quick, sly glance over her shoulder one morning she changed his place in the larder, and hung him up in a darker corner all to himself. Surely, surely, this must mean, John thought, that she wished to keep him as long as she could from sharing her master's table. John did his best to croak his thanks, but was uncertain if the larder maid had heard.

This was one happy thing. His other joy was this. Almost as soon as he found himself safe in his corner, he had discovered that on a level with his head there stood on a shelf a number of jars and gallipots and jorams of glass and earthenware. In some were dried roots, in some what seemed to be

hanks of grass, in others black-veined lily bulbs, or scraps of twig, or dried-up buds and leaves, like tea. John guessed they must be savourings his cookmaid kept for the Fish Lord to soak his fish in, and wondered sadly which, when his own turn came, would be his. But a little apart from the rest and not above eighteen inches from his nose, there stood yet another small glass jar, with greenish stuff inside it. And after many attempts and often with eyes too dry to read, John spelled out at last from the label of this jar these outlandish words:

UNGUENTUM AD PISCES
HOMINIBUS
TRANSMOGRIFICANDOS.

And he went over them again and again until he knew them by heart.

Now John had left school very early. He had taken up crow-scaring at seven, pig-keeping at nine, turnip-hoeing at twelve – though he had kept up none of them for very long. But even if John had stayed at school until he was grown-up, he would never have learned any Latin – none at all, not even dog Latin – since the old dame who kept the village school at Tussock didn't know any herself. She could cut and come again as easily as you please with the cane she kept in her cupboard, but this had never done John much good, and she didn't know any Latin.

John's only certainty then, even

when he had learned these words by heart, was that they were not good honest English words. Still, he had his wits about him. He remembered that there had been words like these written in red on the parchment over the top of the rhyme that now must be where his breeches were, since he had tucked it into his pocket – though where *that* was he hadn't the least notion. But *unguent* was a word he now knew as well as his own name; and it meant ointment. Not many months before this, too, he had mended a chair for a great lady that lived in a high house on the village green – a queer lady too though she was the youngest daughter of a marquis of those parts. It was a job that had not taken John very long, and she was mightily pleased with it. "Sakes, John," she had said, when he had taken the chair back and put it down in the light of a window, "sakes, John, what a *transmogrification*!" And John had blushed all over as he grinned back at the lady, guessing that she meant that the chair showed a change for the better.

Then, too, when he was a little boy, his mother had often told him tales of the piskies. "Piskies, PISCES," muttered John to himself on his hook. It sounded even to his ear poor spelling, but it would do. Then too, HOMINIBUS. If you make a full round O of the first syllable it sounds uncommonly like *home*. So what the Lord Fish, John thought at last, had meant by this lingo on his glass pot must be

that it contained an UNGUENT
to which some secret PISKY stuff
or what is known as wizardry
had been added, and that it
was useful for "changing" for the
better anything or anybody
on which it was rubbed when
away from HOME. Nobody could
call the stony cell in which
the enchanted maid with the
fishtail was kept shut up a
home; and John himself at this
moment was a good many miles
from his mother!

Besides, the stuff in the glass
pot was uncommonly like the
ointment which he had taken
from the other pot and had
smeared on his ribs. After all this
thinking John was just clever
enough to come to the conclusion
that the one unguent had been

meant for turning humans into fish, and that this in the pot beside him was for turning fish into humans again. At this his flat eyes bulged indeed in his head, and in spite of the moss around them his fins stood out stiff as knitting needles. He gasped to himself — like a tench out of water. And while he was still brooding on his discovery, the larder maid opened the door of the larder with her iron key to set about her morning duties.

"*Ackh*," she called softly, hastening towards him, for now she never failed to visit him first of all her charges, "*ackh*, what's wrong with 'ee? What's amiss with 'ee?" and with her lean finger she gently stroked the top of his head, her narrow bony face crooked up

with care at seeing this sudden
change in his looks. She did not
realize that it was not merely a
change but a transmogrification!
She sprinkled him twice, and yet
a third time, with her ice-cold
water, and with the tips of her
small fingers pushed tiny
gobbet after gobbet
of milkpap out of
her basin into

his mouth until John could swallow no more. Then with gaspings and gapings he fixed his nearer eye on the jar of unguent or ointment, gazed back rapidly at the little larder maid, then once again upon the jar.

Now this larder maid was a great-grandniece of the Lord Fish, and had learned a little magic. "Aha," she whispered, smiling softly and wagging her finger at him. "So that's what you are after, Master Tench? That's what you are after, you crafty Master Sobersides. Oh, what a scare you gave me!"

Her words rang out shrill as a whistle, and John's fellow fish, trussed up around him in their moss and grass and rushes on their dishes, or dangling from their hooks, trembled at sound of it.

A faint chuffling, a lisping and quiet gaggling, tiny squeaks and groans filled the larder. John had heard these small noises before, and had supposed them to be fish talk, but though he had tried to imitate them he had never been sure of an answer. All he could do, then, was what he had done before – he fixed again his round glassy eye first on the jar and then on the little larder maid, and this with as much gentle flattery and affection as he could manage. Just as when he was a child at his mother's knee he would coax her to give him a slice of bread pudding or a spoonful of jam.

"Now I wonder," muttered the larder maid as if to herself, "if you, my dear, are the one kind or the other. And if you are the *other*, *shall* I, my gold-green Tinker, take the top off the jar?"

At this John wriggled might and main, chapping with his jaws as wide and loud as he could, looking indeed as if at any moment he might burst into song.

"Ah," cried the maid, watching him with delight, "he understands! That he does! But if I did, precious, what would my lord the Lord Fish say to me? What would happen to *me*, eh? You, Master Tench, I am afraid, are thinking only of your own comfort."

At this John sighed and hung limp as if in sadness and dudgeon and remorse. The larder maid eyed him a few moments longer, then set about her morning work so quickly and with so intense a look on her lean narrow face, with its lank dangling tresses of green-grey hair, that between hope and fear John hardly knew how to contain himself. And while she worked on, sprinkling, feeding, scouring, dipping, she spoke to her charges in much the same way that a groom talks to his horses, a nurse to a baby, or a man to his dogs. At last, her work over, she hastened out of the larder and shut the door.

Now it was the habit of the Lord Fish on the Tuesdays, Thursdays and Saturdays of every week, to make the round of his larder, eyeing all it held, plump fish or puny, old or new, ailing or active; sometimes gently pushing his finger in under the moss to see how they were prospering for his table. This was a Thursday. And sure enough the larder maid presently hastened back, and coming close whispered up at John, "Hst, he comes! The Lord Fish! Angry and hungry. Beware! Stay mum as mum can be, you precious thing. Flat and limp and sulky, look 'ee, for if the Lord Fish makes his choice of 'ee now, it is too late and all is over. And above all things, don't so much as goggle for a moment at that jar!"

She was out again like a swallow at nesting time, and presently there came the sound of slow scraping footsteps on the flag-stones and there entered the Lord Fish into the larder, the maid at his heels. He was no lord to look at, thought John; no marquis, anyhow. He looked as glum and sullen as some old Lenten cod in a fishmonger's, in his stiff drab-coloured overclothes. And John hardly dared to breathe, but hung — mouth open and eyes fixed — as limp and lifeless from his hook in the ceiling as he knew how.

"*Hoy, hoy, hoy*," grumbled the Lord Fish, when at last he came into John's corner. "Here's a dullard. Here's a rack of bones. Here's a sandy gristle-trap. Here's a good-as-dead-and-gone-and-useless! Ay, now my dear, you can't have seen him. Not this one. You must have let him go by, up there in the shadows. A quick eye, my dear, a quick watchful eye! He's naught but muddy sluggard tench 'tis true. But, oh yes, we can better him! He wants life, he wants exercise, he wants

cosseting and feeding and *fattening*.
And then – why then, there's the
makings in him of as comely a
platter of fish as would satisfy
my Lord Bishop of the Seven
Sturgeons himself." And the
little larder maid, her one hand
clutching a swab of moss and the
other demurely knuckled over her
mouth, sedately nodded.

"Ay, master," said she, "he's
hung up there in the shadows, he
is. In the dark. He's a mumper,
that one, he's a moper. He takes
his pap but poorly. He shall have a
washabout and a dose of sunshine
in the trough. Trust me, master,
I'll soon put a little life into him.
Come next Saturday, now!"

"So, so, so," said the Lord Fish.
And having made the round of
John's companions he retired at

last from out of his larder, well content with his morning's visit. And with but one quick reassuring nod at John over her narrow shoulder, his nimble larder maid followed after him. John was safe until Saturday.

Hardly had the Lord Fish's scuffling footsteps died away when back came the little maid, wringing her hands in glee, and scarcely able to speak for laughing. "Ay, Master Tench, did you hear that? 'Up there in the shadows. Here's a dullard; here's a rack of bones; here's a gristle-trap. He wants cosseting and feeding and fattening.' – Did he not now? Was I sly? Was I cunning? Did the old Lord nibble my bait, Master Tench? Did he *not* now? Oho, my poor beautiful; 'fatten', indeed!"

And she lightly stroked John's snout again. "What's wrong with the old Lord Fish is that he eats too much and sleeps too long. Come 'ee now, let's make no more ado about it."

She dragged up a wooden stool that stood close by, and, holding her breath, with both hands she carefully lifted down the jar of green fat or grease or unguent. Then she unlatched John from his hook, and laid him gently on the stone slab beside her, bidding him meanwhile have no fear at all of what might happen. She stripped off his verdant coat of moss, and, dipping her finger in the ointment, smeared it on him, from the nape of his neck clean down his spine to the very tip of his tail.

For a few moments John felt like a cork that, after bobbing softly along down a softly flowing river, is suddenly drawn into a roaring whirlpool. He felt like a firework squib when the gushing sparks are nearly all out of it and it is about to burst. Then gradually the fog in his eyes and the clamour in his ears faded and waned away, and lo and behold, he found himself returned safe and sound into his own skin, shape and appearance again. There he stood in the Lord Fish's fish larder, grinning down out of his cheerful face at the maid who in stature reached not much above his elbow.

"Ah," she cried, peering up at him out of her small water-clear eyes, and a little dazed and dazzled herself at this transmogrification.

"So you *were* the other kind, Master Tench!" And the larder maid looked at him so sorrowfully and fondly that poor John could only blush and turn away. "And now," she continued, "all you will be wanting, I suppose, is to be gone. I beseech you then make haste and be off, or my own skin will pay for it."

John had always been a dullard with words. But he thanked the larder maid for all she had done for him as best he could. And he slipped from off his little finger a silver ring which had belonged to his father, and put it into the palm of the larder maid's hand; for just as when he had been changed into a fish, all his clothes and everything about him had become fish itself, so now when

he was transformed into human shape again, all that had then been his returned into its own place, even to the parchment in his breeches' pocket. Such it seems is the law of enchantment. And he entreated the maid, if ever she should find herself on the other side of the great wall, to ask for the village of Tussock, and when she came to Tussock to ask for Mrs Cobbler.

"That's my mother," said John, "is Mrs Cobbler. And she'll be mighty pleased to see you, I promise you. And so will I."

The larder maid looked at John. Then she took the ring between finger and thumb, and with a sigh pushed it into a cranny between the slabs of stone for a hiding-place. "Stay there," she whispered to the ring, "and I'll come back to 'ee anon."

Then John, having nothing else handy, and knowing that for the larder maid's sake he must leave the pot behind him, took out of the fob in his breeches' pocket a great silver watch that had belonged to his grandfather. It was nothing now but a watch *case*, since he had one day taken out the works in hopes to make it go better, and had been too lazy to put them back again. Into this case he smeared as much of the grease out of the pot as it would hold.

"And now, Master Tench, this way," said the larder maid, twisting round on him. "You must be going, and you must be going for good. Follow that wall as far as it leads you, and then cross the garden where the Lord Fish grows his herbs. You will know it by the scent of them in the air. Climb the wall and go on until you come to the river. Swim across that, and turn sunwards while it is morning. The Lord Fish has the nose of a she-wolf. He'd smell 'ee out across a bean field. Get you gone at once then, and meddle with him no more. Ay, and I know it is not on me your thoughts will be thinking when you get to safety again."

John, knowing no other, stooped down and kissed this little wiseacre's lean cold fingers, and casting one helpless and doleful look all about the larder at the fish on hook and slab, and seeing none, he fancied, that could possibly be in the same state as his had been, he hastened out.

There was no missing his way. The Lord Fish's walls and water conduits were all of stone so solid that they might have been built by the Romans, though, truly, they were chiefly of magic, which has nothing to do with time. John hurried along in the morning sunshine, and came at length to the stream. With his silver watch between his teeth for safety he swam to the other side. Here grew very tall rough spiny reeds and grasses, some seven to nine feet high. He pushed his way through them, heedless of their clawing and rasping, and only just in time. For as soon as he was safely hidden in the low bushes beyond them, whom did he now see approaching on the other side of the stream, rod in hand, and creel at his elbow, but the Lord Fish himself − his lank face erected up into the air and his nose sniffing the morning as if it were laden with the spices of Arabia. The larder maid had told the truth indeed. For at least an hour the Lord Fish stood there motionless on the other side of the stream immediately opposite John's hiding-place. For at least an hour he pried and peeped about him, gently sniffing on. And, though teased by flies and stung with nettles, John dared not stir a finger. At last even the Lord Fish grew weary of watching and waiting, and John, having seen him well out of sight, continued on his way.

What more is there to tell? Sad and sorrowful had been the maid's waiting for him, sad beyond anything else in the fish-tailed damsel's memory. For, ever since she had so promised him, she had

not even been able to sing to keep herself company. But when seventeen days after he had vanished, John plunged in again under the stone arch and climbed the steep stone steps to her chamber, he spent no time in trying to find words and speeches that would not come. Having opened the glass of his watch, he just knelt down beside her, and said, "*Now*, if you please, lady. If you can keep quite still, I will be quick. If only I could bear the pain I'd do it three times over, but I promise 'ee it's soon gone." And with his finger he gently smeared the magic unguent on the maid's tail down at last to the very tip.

Life is full of curiosities, and curious indeed it was that though at one moment John's talk to the enchanted creature had seemed to her little better than Double Dutch, and she could do his bidding only by the signs he had made to her, at the next they were chattering together as merrily as if they had done nothing else all their lives. But they did not talk for long, since of a sudden there came the clatter of oars, and presently a skinny hand was thrust over the window-sill, and her daily portion of bread and fruit and water was laid out on the sill. The sound of the Lord Fish's "Halloo!" when he had lowered his basket into the boat made the blood run cold again in John's body. He waited only until the rap and grinding of the oars had died away. Then he took the maid by the hand, and they went down the stone steps together. There they plunged into the dark water, and presently found themselves breathless but happy beyond words seated together on the green grass bank in the afternoon sunshine. And there came such a chattering and cawing from the rooks and jackdaws over their heads that it seemed as if they were giving thanks to see them there. And when John had shaken out the coat he had left under the tree seventeen days before, brushed off the mildew, and dried it in the sun, he put it over the maid's shoulders.

It was long after dark when they came to Tussock, and not a soul was to be seen in the village street or on the green. John looked in through the window at his mother. She sat alone by the hearthside, staring into the fire, and it seemed to her that she would never get warm again. When John came in and she was clasped in his arms, first she thought she was going to faint then she began to cry a little, and then to scold him as she had never scolded him before. John dried her tears and hushed her scoldings. And when he had told her a little of his story, he brought the maid in. And John's mother first bobbed her a curtsy, then kissed her and made her welcome. And she listened to John's story all over again from the beginning to the end before they went to bed – though John's bed that night was an old armchair.

Now before the bells of Tussock church – which was a small one and old – rang out a peal for John's and the fish maid's wedding, he set off as early as ever one morning to climb the wall again. In their haste to be gone from the Sorcerer's mansion she had left her belongings behind her, and particularly, she told John, a leaden box or casket, stamped with a great A – for Almanara; that being her name.

Very warily John stripped again, and, diving quietly, swam in under the stone arch. And lo, safe and sound, in the far corner of the room of all her grief and captivity, stood the leaden casket. But when he stooped to lift it, his troubles began. It was exceedingly heavy, and to swim with it even on his shoulders would be to swim to the bottom! He sat awhile and pondered, and at last climbed up to the stone window, carved curiously with flowers and birds and fish, and looked out. Water lay beneath him in a moat afloat with lilies, though he couldn't tell how deep. But by good fortune a knotted rope hung from a hook in the window-sill − for the use, no doubt, of the Lord Fish in his boat. John hauled the rope in, tied one end of it to the ring in the leaden casket and one to a small wooden stool. At last after long heaving and hoisting he managed to haul the casket on to the sill.

He pushed it
over, and — as
lively as a small
pig — away went the
stool after it. John clambered up
to the window again and again
looked out. The stool, still
bobbing, floated on the water
beneath him. Only a deeper quiet
had followed the splash of the
casket. So, after he had dragged
it out of the moat and on to the
bank, John ventured on beyond

the walls of the great house in search of the Lord Fish's larder. He dearly wanted to thank the larder maid again. When at last he found it, it was all shut up and deserted. He climbed up to the window and looked in, but quickly jumped down again, for every fish that hung inside it hung dead as mutton. The little larder maid was gone. But whether she had first used the magic unguent on the Lord Fish himself and then in dismay of what followed had run away, or whether she had tried it on them both and now was what John couldn't guess, he never knew and could never discover. He grieved not to see her again, and always thought of her with kindness.

Walking and resting, walking and resting, it took him
three days, even though
he managed to borrow
a wheelbarrow for the
last two miles, to get
the casket home.
But it was worth
the trouble.

When he managed at last to prise the lid open, it was as though lumps of a frozen rainbow had suddenly spilled over in the kitchen, the casket was crammed so full of precious stones. And after the wedding Almanara had a great J punched into the lead of the box immediately after her great A − since now what it held belonged to them both.

But though John was now married, and not only less idle but as happy as a kingfisher, *still* when the sweet south wind came blowing, and the leaves were green on the trees, and the birds in song, he could not keep his thoughts from hankering after water. So sometimes he made himself a little paste or dug up a few worms, and went off fishing.

But he made two rules for himself, First, whenever he hooked anything – and especially a tench – he would always smear a speck or two of the unguent out of his grandfather's silver watch case on the top of its head; and next, having made sure that his fish was fish, wholly fish, and nothing but fish, he would put it back into the water again. As for the mansion of the Sorcerer, he had made a vow to Almanara and to his mother that he would never go fishing *there*. And he never did.

To David Burnett

P.B.

Other books in this series

The Canterville Ghost
Elsie Piddock Skips in Her Sleep
Little Long-nose
Rikki-tikki-tavi
A White Heron

First published 1997 by Walker Books Ltd
87 Vauxhall Walk, London SE11 5HJ

2 4 6 8 10 9 7 5 3 1

Text © 1993, 1997 Walter de la Mare
Illustrations © 1997 Patrick Benson

This book has been typeset in M Bembo.

Printed in Italy

British Library Cataloguing in Publication Data
A catalogue record for this book is available
from the British Library.

ISBN 0-7445-4947-7